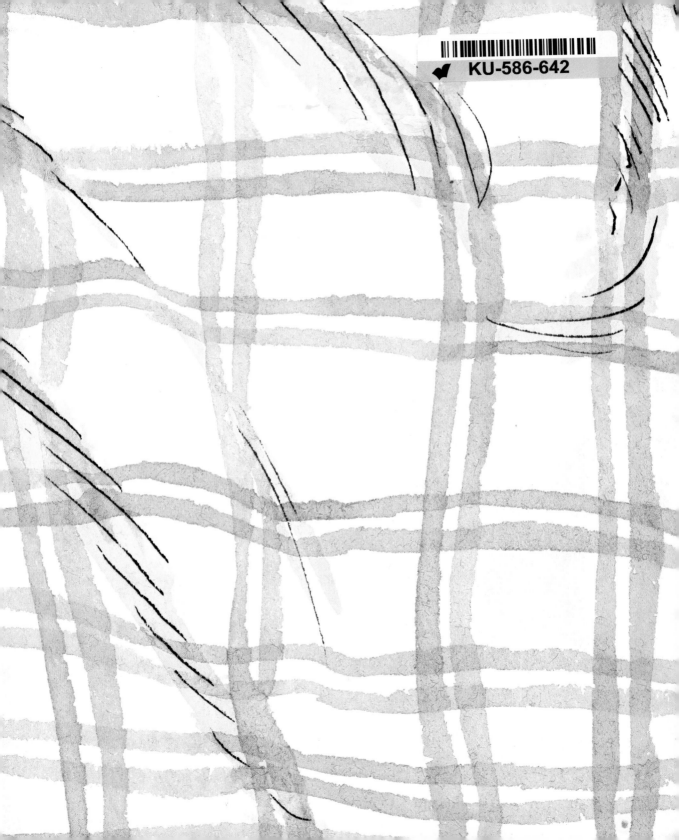

For Jean Pierre

First published 1986 by
Walker Books Ltd
87 Vauxhall Walk
London SE11 5HJ

This edition published 1996

2 4 6 8 10 9 7 5 3 1

© 1986 Chris Riddell

Printed in Hong Kong

British Library Cataloguing in Publication Data
A catalogue record for this book is available
from the British Library.

ISBN 0-7445-5504-3

BEN AND THE BEAR

written and illustrated by
Chris Riddell

WALKER BOOKS
AND SUBSIDIARIES
LONDON · BOSTON · SYDNEY

One day Ben was bored.

He put on a big winter coat.

He put on a floppy hat.

Then he set off into the snow.

After a while he met a bear.
The bear said,
'What a lovely coat.'
Ben said, 'Come home for tea.'

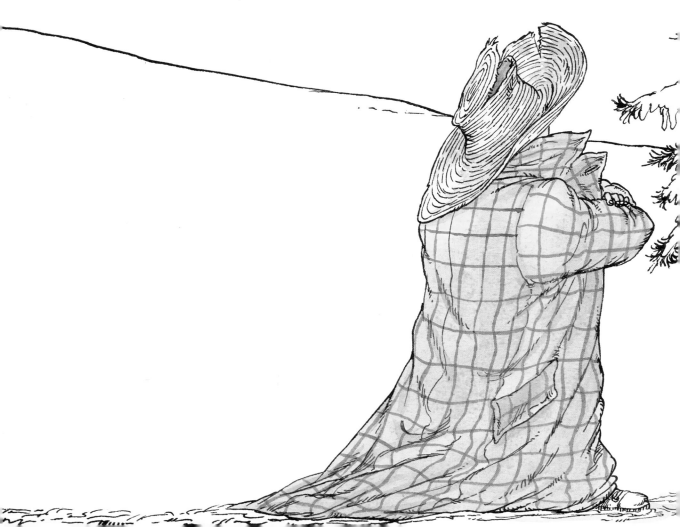

Some of the way

the bear carried Ben.

Some of the way
Ben tried to carry the bear.

The bear took Ben's coat.

Ben and the bear
sat down at the table.

The bear poured the tea.

Ben passed the sugar lumps.
The bear ate them all up.

They ate some bread.

And then they ate some honey.

The bear said, 'Let's dance.'
So they did.

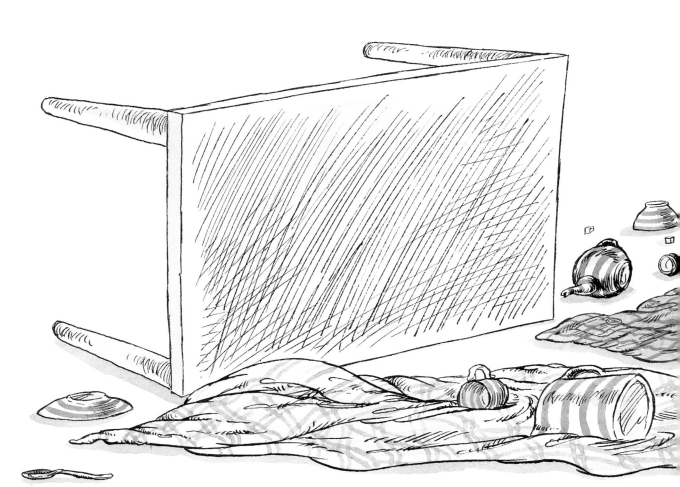

Ben said, 'What a mess!'
The bear said,
'Let's play tidying up.'

They did the washing up.

They put the dishes away.

They folded the tablecloth.

Ben said, 'That looks tidy.'
The bear said,
'What about the coat?'

Ben said,

'You can have the coat.'

The bear said, 'Tomorrow you must come to tea at my house.'

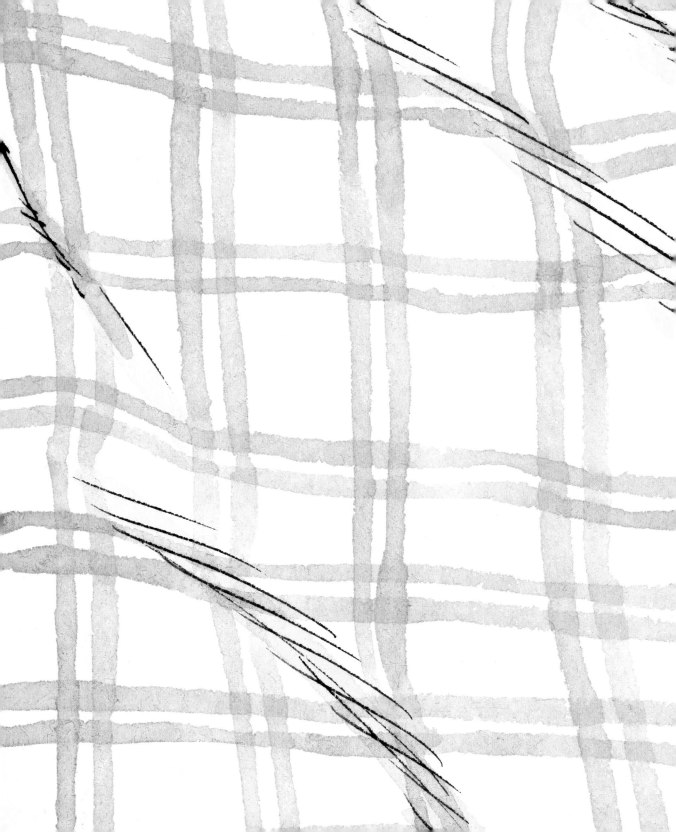